Agatha Christie Short Story Fiction Collection:
The Million Dollar Bond Robbery, Jewel Robbery at the Grand Metropolitan, Adventure of the Egyptian Tomb, and The Kidnapped Prime Minister

D1525420

By: Agatha Christie

TABLE OF CONTENTS

THE MILLION DOLLAR BOND ROBBERY

WHAT a number of bond robberies there have been lately," I observed one morning, laying aside the newspaper. "Poirot, let us forsake the science of detection and take to crime instead."

"You are on the — how do you say it? — get-rich-quick tack, eh, mon ami?"

"Well, look at this last coup — the million dollars' worth of Liberty Bonds which the London and Scottish Bank were sending to New York, and which disappeared in such a remarkable manner on board the Olympia."

"If it were not for the mal de mer — and the difficulty of practising the so excellent method of Laverguier for a longer time than the few hours of crossing the Channel — I should delight to voyage myself on one of these big liners," murmured Poirot dreamily.

"Yes indeed!" I said enthusiastically. "Some of them must be perfect palaces; the swimming-baths, the lounges, the restaurants, the palm courts — really, it must be hard to believe that one is on the sea."

"Me, I always know when I am on the sea," said Poirot sadly. "And all those bagatelles that you enumerate, they say nothing to me; but, my friend, consider for a moment the geniuses that travel, as it were, incognito! On board these floating palaces, as you so justly call them, one would meet the élite, the haute noblesse of the criminal world!"
I laughed.

"So that's the way your enthusiasm runs. You would have liked to cross swords with the man who sneaked the Liberty Bonds?"

The landlady interrupted us.

"A young lady as wants to see you, Mr. Poirot. Here's her card."

The card bore the inscription, "Miss Esmé Farquhar," and Poirot, after diving under the table to retrieve a stray crumb, nodded to the landlady to admit her.

In another minute one of the most charming girls I have ever seen was ushered into the room. She was, perhaps, about five-and-twenty, with big brown eyes and a perfect figure. She was well dressed, and perfectly composed in manner.

"Sit down, I beg of you, Mademoiselle. This is my friend Captain Hastings, who aids me in my little problems."
"I am afraid it is a big problem I have brought you to-day, M. Poirot," said the girl, giving me a pleasant bow as she seated herself. "I daresay you have read about it in the papers. I am referring to the theft of Liberty Bonds on the Olympia."
Some astonishment must have shown itself in Poirot's face, for she continued quickly —

"You are doubtless asking yourself what I have to do with a grave institution like the London and Scottish Bank. In one sense, nothing; in another sense, everything. You see, M. Poirot, I am engaged to Mr. Philip Ridgeway."
"Aha! And Mr. Philip Ridgeway — —"

"Was in charge of the bonds when they were stolen. Of course, no actual blame can attach to him; it was not his fault in any way. Nevertheless, he is half-distraught over the matter, and his uncle, I know, insists that he must carelessly have mentioned having them in his possession. It is a terrible setback in his career."

"Who is his uncle?"

"Mr. Vavasour, joint general manager of the London and Scottish Bank."

"Suppose, Miss Farquhar, that you recount to me the whole story?"

"Very well. As you know, the bank wished to extend their credits in America, and for this purpose decided to send over a million dollars in Liberty Bonds. Mr. Vavasour selected his nephew, who had occupied a position of trust in the bank for many years, and was conversant with all the details of the bank's dealings in New York, to make the trip. The Olympia sailed from Liverpool on the 23rd, and the bonds were handed over to Philip on the morning of that day by Mr. Vavasour and Mr. Shaw — the two joint general managers of the London and Scottish. They were counted, enclosed in a package, and sealed in his presence, and he then locked the package at once in his portmanteau."

"A portmanteau with an ordinary lock?"

"No; Mr. Shaw insisted on a special lock being fitted to it by Messrs. Hubbs. Philip, as I say, placed the package at the bottom of the trunk. It was stolen just a few hours before reaching New York. A rigorous search of the whole ship was made, but without result. The bonds seemed literally to vanish into thin air."

Poirot made a grimace.

"But they did not vanish absolutely, since I gather that they were sold in small parcels within half-an-hour of the docking of the Olympia! Well, undoubtedly the next thing is for me to see Mr. Ridgeway."

"I was about to suggest that you should lunch with me at the Cheshire Cheese. Philip will be there. He is meeting me, but does not yet know that I have been consulting you on his behalf."

Philip Ridgeway was a pleasant-faced man of thirty-odd, with just a touch of greying hair at the temples. His face looked drawn and haggard. The theft of the bonds which had been placed in his charge had almost demoralised him, and he reproached himself vainly for not having exercised greater care. Over the excellent steak-and-kidney pudding of the establishment he confirmed his fiancée's story in every particular. Poirot then proceeded to question him.
"What led you to discover that the bonds had been stolen, M. Ridgeway?"

The man laughed rather bitterly.

"The thing stared me in the face, M. Poirot—I couldn't have missed it. My cabin trunk was half out from under the bunk, and all scratched and cut about where they'd tried to force the lock."

"But I understood that it had been opened with a key?"
"That's so. They tried to force it, but couldn't. And in the end they got it unlocked somehow."

"Curious," said Poirot, his eyes beginning to flicker with the green light that I knew so well. "Very curious! They waste much time trying to prise it open, and then, sapristi! they find they have the key all the time—for each of Messrs. Hubbs' locks is unique!"

"They couldn't have had the key. It never left me day or night."

"You are sure of that?"

"I can swear to it, and, besides, if they had had the key or a duplicate, why should they waste time trying to force an obviously unforceable lock?"

"Ah, there is exactly the question we are asking ourselves! You will see, the solution, if we ever find it, will hinge on that curious fact. I beg of you not to assault me if I ask you one more question: Are you perfectly certain you did not leave the trunk unlocked?"

Philip Ridgeway merely looked at him, and Poirot gesticulated apologetically.

"Ah, but these things can happen, I assure you! Very well; the bonds were stolen from the trunk. What did the thief do with them? How did he manage to get ashore with them?"

"Ah!" cried Ridgeway. "That's just it. How? Word was passed to the Customs authorities, and every soul that left the ship was gone over with a tooth-comb!"

"And the bonds, I gather, made a bulky package?"

"Certainly they did. They could hardly have been hidden on board—and, anyway, we know they weren't, because they were offered for sale within half-an-hour of the Olympia's arrival, long before I got the cables going and the numbers sent out. One broker swears he bought some of them even before the Olympia got in! But you can't send bonds by wireless!"

"Not by wireless; but did any tug come alongside?"

"Only the official ones, and that was after the alarm was given, when everyone was on the look-out. I was watching out myself for their being passed over to someone that way. My God, M. Poirot, this thing will drive me mad! People are beginning to say I stole them myself."

"But you also were searched on landing, were you not?" asked Poirot gently.

"Yes."

The young man stared at him in a puzzled manner.

"You do not catch my meaning, I see," said Poirot, smiling enigmatically. "Now I should like to make a few inquiries at the bank."

Ridgeway produced a card and scribbled a few words on it. "Send this in, and my uncle will see you at once."

Poirot thanked him, bade farewell to Miss Farquhar, and together we started out for Threadneedle Street and the head office of the London and Scottish Bank. On production of Ridgeway's card we were led through the labyrinth of counters and desks, skirting paying-in clerks and paying-out clerks, and up to a small office on the first floor, where the joint general managers received us. They were two grave gentlemen, who had grown grey in the service of the bank. Mr. Vavasour had a short white beard, Mr. Shaw was clean-shaven.

"I understand you are strictly a private inquiry agent?" said Mr. Vavasour. "Quite so, quite so. We have, of course, placed ourselves in the hands of Scotland Yard. Inspector McNeil has charge of the case. A very able officer, I believe."

"I am sure of it," said Poirot politely. "You will permit a few questions, on your nephew's behalf? About this lock—who ordered it from Messrs. Hubbs?"

"I ordered it myself," said Mr. Shaw. "I would not trust to any clerk in the matter. As to the keys, Mr. Ridgeway had one, and the other two are held by my colleague and myself."
"And no clerk has had access to them?"

Mr. Shaw turned inquiringly to Mr. Vavasour.

"I think I am correct in saying that they have remained in the safe where we placed them on the twenty-third," said Mr. Vavasour, and then added: "My colleague was unfortunately taken ill a fortnight ago—in fact, on the very day that Philip left us. He has only just recovered."

"Severe bronchitis is no joke to a man of my age," said Mr. Shaw ruefully. "But I am afraid Mr. Vavasour has suffered from the hard work entailed by my absence, especially with this unexpected worry coming on top of everything."
Poirot asked a few more questions. I judged that he was endeavouring to gauge the exact amount of intimacy between uncle and nephew. Mr. Vavasour's answers were brief and punctilious. His nephew was a trusted official of the Bank, and had no debts or money difficulties that he knew of. He had been entrusted with similar missions in the past. Finally we were politely bowed out.

"I am disappointed," said Poirot as we emerged into the street. "You hoped to discover more? They are such stodgy old men."

"It is not their stodginess which disappoints me, mon ami. I do not expect to find in a bank manager a 'keen financier with an eagle glance,' as your favourite works of fiction put it. No, I am disappointed in the case—it is too easy!"

"Easy?"

"Yes, do you not find it almost childishly simple?"

"You know who stole the bonds?"

"I do."

"But then—we must—why——"

"Do not confuse and fluster yourself, Hastings. We are not going to do anything at present."

"But why? What are you waiting for?"

"For the Olympia. She is due on her return trip from New York on Tuesday."

"But if you know who stole the bonds, why wait? He may escape."

"To a South Sea Island, where there is no extradition? No, mon ami, he would find life very uncongenial there. As to why I wait—eh bien! To the intelligence of Hercule Poirot the case is perfectly clear; but for the benefit of others not so greatly gifted by the good God—the Inspector McNeil, for instance—it would be as well to make a few inquiries to establish the facts. One must have consideration for those less gifted than oneself."

"Good Lord, Poirot! Do you know, I'd give a considerable sum of money to see you make a thorough ass of yourself—just for once. You're so confoundedly conceited!"

"Do not enrage yourself, Hastings. In verity, I observe that there are times when you almost detest me! Alas! I suffer the penalties of greatness!"

The little man puffed out his chest and sighed so comically that I was forced to laugh.

Tuesday saw us speeding to Liverpool in a first-class carriage of the L. and N.W.R. Poirot had obstinately refused to enlighten me as to his suspicions—or certainties. He contented himself with expressing surprise that I, too, was not equally au fait with the situation. I disdained to argue and entrenched my curiosity behind a rampart of pretended indifference. Once arrived at the quay alongside which lay the big Transatlantic liner, Poirot became brisk and alert. Our proceedings consisted in interviewing four successive stewards and inquiring after a friend of Poirot's who had crossed to New York on the 23rd.

"An elderly gentleman, wearing glasses. A great invalid, hardly moved out of his cabin."

The description appeared to tally with one Mr. Ventnor, who had occupied the cabin C24, which was next to that of Philip Ridgeway. Although unable to see how Poirot had deduced Mr. Ventnor's existence and personal appearance, I was keenly excited.

"Tell me," I cried, "was this gentleman one of the first to land when you got to New York?"

The steward shook his head.

"No, indeed, Sir. He was one of the last off the boat."

I retired crestfallen, and observed Poirot grinning at me. He thanked the steward, a note changed hands, and we took our departure.

"It's all very well," I remarked heatedly; "but that last answer must have damped your precious theory, grin as you please!"
"As usual, you see nothing, Hastings. That last answer is, on the contrary, the coping stone of my theory."
I flung up my hands in despair.

"I give it up."

• ☐ • ☐ • ☐ • ☐ •

Once more we were in a train—speeding towards London this time. Poirot wrote busily for a few minutes, and then sealed up the result in an envelope.

"This is for the good Inspector McNeil. We will leave it at Scotland Yard in passing, and then to the Rendez-Vous Restaurant, where I have asked Miss Esmé Farquhar to do us the honour of dining with us."

"What about Ridgeway?"

"What about him?" asked Poirot, with a twinkle.

"Why, you surely don't think—you can't——"

"The habit of incoherence is growing upon you, Hastings. As a matter of fact, I did think. If Ridgeway had been the thief (which was perfectly possible) the case would have been charming—a piece of neat, methodical work."

"But not so charming for Miss Farquhar."

"Possibly you are right. Therefore, all is for the best. Now, Hastings, let us review the case. The sealed package is removed from the trunk and vanishes, as Miss Farquhar puts it, into thin air. We will dismiss the thin air theory, which is not practicable at the present stage of science, and consider what is likely to have become of it. Everyone asserts the incredibility of its being smuggled ashore — —"

"Yes, but we know — —"

"You may know, Hastings. I do not. I take the view that, since it seemed incredible, it was incredible. Two possibilities remain. It was hidden on board — also rather difficult; or — it was thrown overboard."

"With a cork on it, do you mean?"

"Without a cork."

I stared.

"But if the bonds were thrown overboard, they could not have been sold in New York."

"I admire your logical mind, Hastings. The bonds were sold in New York; therefore they were not thrown overboard. You see where that leads us?"

"Where we were when we started."

"Jamais de la vie! If the package was thrown overboard and the bonds were sold in New York, the package could not have contained the bonds. Is there any evidence that the package did contain the bonds? Mr. Ridgeway never opened it from the time it was placed in his hands in London."

"Yes, but then — —"

Poirot waved an impatient hand.

"Permit me to continue. The last moment that the bonds are seen as bonds is in the office of the London and Scottish Bank on the morning of the twenty-third. They reappear in New York half-an-hour after the Olympia gets in, and, according to one man whom nobody listens to, actually before she gets in. Supposing, then, that they have never been on the Olympia at all. Is there any other way they could get to New York? Yes. The Gigantic leaves from Southampton on the same day as the Olympia starts from Liverpool, and the former holds the record for the Atlantic. Mailed by the Gigantic, the bonds would be in New York the day before the Olympia arrived. All is clear; the case begins to explain itself. The sealed package is only a dummy. It would have been an easy matter for any of the three men present to prepare a duplicate package which could be substituted for the genuine one. Très bien, the bonds are mailed to a confederate in New York, with instructions to sell as soon as the Olympia is in; but someone must travel on the Olympia to engineer the supposed moment of the robbery."

"*But why?*"

"Because, if Ridgeway merely opens the packet and finds it a dummy, suspicion flies at once to London. No; the man on board in the cabin next door does his work, pretends to force the lock in an obvious manner so as to draw immediate attention to the theft, really unlocks the trunk with a duplicate key, throws the package overboard, and waits until the last to leave the boat. Naturally, he wears glasses to conceal his eyes, and is an invalid, since he does not want to run the risk of meeting Ridgeway. He steps ashore in New York, and returns by the first boat available."

"But who—which was he?"

"The man who had a duplicate key, the man who ordered the lock, the man who has not been severely ill with bronchitis at his home in the country—enfin, that stodgy old man, Mr. Shaw! There are criminals in high places sometimes, my friend. Ah, here we are! Mademoiselle, I have succeeded! You permit?"

And, beaming, Poirot kissed the astonished girl lightly on either cheek!

THE END.

THE JEWEL ROBBERY AT THE GRAND METROPOLITAN

"Poirot," I said, "a change of air would do you good."

"You think so, mon ami?"

"I am sure of it."

"Eh—eh?" said my friend, smiling. "It is all arranged, then?"

"You will come?"

"Where do you propose to take me?"

"Brighton. As a matter of fact, a friend of mine in the City put me on to a very good thing, and—well, I have money to burn, as the saying goes. I think a weekend at the Grand Metropolitan would do us all the good in the world."

"Thank you, I accept most gratefully. You have the good heart to think of an old man. And the good heart, it is in the end worth all the little grey cells. Yes, yes, I who speak to you am in danger of forgetting that sometimes."

I did not relish the implication. I fancy that Poirot is sometimes a little inclined to underestimate my mental capacities. But his pleasure was so evident that I put my slight annoyance aside.

"Then, that's all right," I said hastily.

Saturday evening saw us dining at the Grand Metropolitan in the midst of a gay throng. All the world and his wife seemed to be at Brighton. The dresses were marvellous, and the jewels — worn sometimes with more love of display than good taste — were something magnificent.

"Hein, it is a good sight, this!" murmured Poirot. "This is the home of the Profiteer, is it not so, Hastings?"

"Supposed to be," I replied. "But we'll hope they aren't all tarred with the Profiteering brush."

Poirot gazed round him placidly.

"The sight of so many jewels makes me wish I had turned my brains to crime, instead of to its detection. What a magnificent opportunity for some thief of distinction! Regard, Hastings, that stout woman by the pillar. She is, as you would say, plastered with gems."

I followed his eyes.

"Why," I exclaimed, "it's Mrs. Opalsen."

"You know her?"

"Slightly. Her husband is a rich stockbroker who made a fortune in the recent oil boom."

After dinner we ran across the Opalsens in the lounge, and I introduced Poirot to them. We chatted for a few minutes, and ended by having our coffee together.

Poirot said a few words in praise of some of the costlier gems displayed on the lady's ample bosom, and she brightened up at once.

"It's a perfect hobby of mine, Mr. Poirot. I just love jewellery. Ed knows my weakness, and every time things go well he brings me something new. You are interested in precious stones?"

"I have had a good deal to do with them one time and another, madame. My profession has brought me into contact with some of the most famous jewels in the world."

He went on to narrate, with discreet pseudonyms, the story of the historic jewels of a reigning house, and Mrs. Opalsen listened with bated breath.

"There now," she exclaimed, as he ended. "If it isn't just like a play! You know, I've got some pearls of my own that have a history attached to them. I believe it's supposed to be one of the finest necklaces in the world — the pearls are so beautifully matched and so perfect in colour. I declare I really must run up and get it!"

"Oh, madame," protested Poirot, "you are too amiable. Pray do not derange yourself!"

"Oh, but I'd like to show it to you."

The buxom dame waddled across to the lift briskly enough. Her husband, who had been talking to me, looked at Poirot inquiringly.

"Madame your wife is so amiable as to insist on showing me her pearl necklace," explained the latter.

"Oh, the pearls!" Opalsen smiled in a satisfied fashion. "Well, they are worth seeing. Cost a pretty penny too! Still, the money's there all right; I could get what I paid for them any day — perhaps more. May have to, too, if things go on as they are now. Money's confoundedly tight in the City. All this infernal EPD." He rambled on, launching into technicalities where I could not follow him.

He was interrupted by a small page boy who approached him and murmured something in his ear.

"Eh—what? I'll come at once. Not taken ill, is she? Excuse me, gentlemen."

He left us abruptly. Poirot leaned back and lit one of his tiny Russian cigarettes. Then, carefully and meticulously, he arranged the empty coffee cups in a neat row, and beamed happily on the result.

The minutes passed. The Opalsens did not return.

"Curious," I remarked, at length. "I wonder when they will come back."

Poirot watched the ascending spirals of smoke, and then said thoughtfully:

"They will not come back."

"Why?"

"Because, my friend, something has happened."

"What sort of thing? How do you know?" I asked curiously.

Poirot smiled.

"A few minutes ago the manager came hurriedly out of his office and ran upstairs. He was much agitated. The liftboy is deep in talk with one of the pages. The lift-bell has rung three times, but he heeds it not. Thirdly, even the waiters are distrait; and to make a waiter distrait—" Poirot shook his head with an air of finality. "The affair must indeed be of the first magnitude. Ah, it is as I thought! Here come the police."

Two men had just entered the hotel—one in uniform, the other in plain clothes. They spoke to a page, and were immediately ushered upstairs. A few minutes later, the same boy descended and came up to where we were sitting.

"Mr. Opalsen's compliments, and would you step upstairs?"

Poirot sprang nimbly to his feet. One would have said that he awaited the summons. I followed with no less alacrity.

The Opalsens' apartments were situated on the first floor. After knocking on the door, the page boy retired, and we answered the summons. "Come in!" A strange scene met our eyes. The room was Mrs. Opalsen's bedroom, and in the centre of it, lying back in an armchair, was the lady herself, weeping violently. She presented an extraordinary spectacle, with the tears making great furrows in the powder with which her complexion was liberally coated. Mr. Opalsen was striding up and down angrily. The two police officials stood in the middle of the room, one with a notebook in hand. An hotel chambermaid, looking frightened to death, stood by the fireplace; and on the other side of the room a Frenchwoman, obviously Mrs. Opalsen's maid, was weeping and wringing her hands, with an intensity of grief that rivalled that of her mistress.

Into this pandemonium stepped Poirot, neat and smiling. Immediately, with an energy surprising in one of her bulk Mrs. Opalsen sprang from her chair towards him.

"There now; Ed may say what he likes, but I believe in luck, I do. It was fated I should meet you the way I did this evening, and I've a feeling that if you can't get my pearls back for me nobody can."

"Calm yourself, I pray of you, madame." Poirot patted her hand soothingly. "Reassure yourself. All will be well. Hercule Poirot will aid you!"

Mr. Opalsen turned to the police inspector.

"There will be no objection to my — er — calling in this gentleman, I suppose?"

"None at all, sir," replied the man civilly, but with complete indifference. "Perhaps now your lady's feeling better she'll just let us have the facts?"

Mrs. Opalsen looked helplessly at Poirot. He led her back to her chair.

"Seat yourself, madame, and recount to us the whole history without agitating yourself."

Thus abjured, Mrs. Opalsen dried her eyes gingerly, and

began.

"I came upstairs after dinner to fetch my pearls for Mr. Poirot here to see. The chambermaid and Célestine were both in the room as usual — "

"Excuse me, madame, but what do you mean by 'as usual?' "

Mr. Opalsen explained.

"I make it a rule that no one is to come into this room unless Célestine, the maid, is there also. The chambermaid does the room in the morning while Célestine is present, and comes in after dinner to turn down the beds under the same conditions; otherwise she never enters the room."

"Well, as I was saying," continued Mrs. Opalsen, "I came up. I went to the drawer here" — she indicated the bottom right-hand drawer of the kneehole dressing table — "took out my jewel case and unlocked it. It seemed quite as usual — but the pearls were not there!"

The inspector had been busy with his notebook. When had you last seen them?" he asked.

"They were there when I went down to dinner."

"You are sure?"

"Quite sure. I was uncertain whether to wear them or not, but in the end I decided on the emeralds, and put them back in the jewel case."

"Who locked up the jewel case?"

"I did. I wear the key on a chain round my neck." She held it up as she spoke.

The inspector examined it, and shrugged his shoulders.

"The thief must have had a duplicate key. No difficult matter. The lock is quite a simple one. What did you do after you'd locked the jewel case?"

"I put it back in the bottom drawer where I always keep it."

"You didn't lock the drawer?"

"No, I never do. My maid remains in the room till I come up, so there's no need."

The inspector's face grew greyer.

"Am I to understand that the jewels were there when you went down to dinner, and that since then the maid has not left the room?"

Suddenly, as though the horror of her own situation for the first time burst upon her, Célestine uttered a piercing shriek, and, flinging herself upon Poirot, poured out a torrent of incoherent French.

The suggestion was infamous! That she should be suspected of robbing Madame! The police were well known to be of a stupidity incredible! But Monsieur, who was a Frenchman—"

"A Belgian," interjected Poirot, but Célestine paid no attention to the correction.

Monsieur would not stand by and see her falsely accused, while that infamous chambermaid was allowed to go scot-free. She had never liked her—a bold, red-faced thing—a born thief. She had said from the first that she was not honest. And had kept a sharp watch over her too, when she was doing Madame's room! Let those idiots of policemen search her, and if they did not find Madame's pearls on her it would be very surprising!

Although this harangue was uttered in rapid and virulent French, Célestine had interlarded it with a wealth of gesture, and the chambermaid realized at least a part of her meaning. She reddened angrily.

"If that foreign woman's saying I took the pearls, it's a lie!" she declared heatedly. "I never so much as saw them."

"Search her!" screamed the other. "You will find it is as

I say."

"You're a lair — do you hear?" said the chambermaid, advancing upon her. "Stole 'em yourself, and want to put it on me. Why, I was only in the room about three minutes before the lady came up, and then you were sitting here the whole time, as you always do, like a cat watching a mouse."

The inspector looked across inquiringly at Célestine. "Is that true? Didn't you leave the room at all?"

"I did not actually leave her alone," admitted Célestine reluctantly, "but I went into my own room through the door here twice — once to fetch a reel of cotton, and once for my scissors. She must have done it then."

"You wasn't gone a minute," retorted the chambermaid angrily. "Just popped out and in again. I'd be glad if the police would search me. I've nothing to be afraid of."

At this moment there was a tap at the door. The inspector went to it. His face brightened when he saw who it was.

"Ah!" he said. "That's rather fortunate. I sent for one of our female searchers, and she's just arrived. Perhaps if you wouldn't mind going into the room next door."

He looked at the chambermaid, who stepped across the threshold with a toss of her head, the searcher following her closely.

The French girl had sunk sobbing into a chair. Poirot was looking round the room, the main features of which I have made clear by a sketch.

"Where does that door lead?" he inquired, nodding his head towards the one by the window.

"Into the next apartment, I believe," said the inspector. "It's bolted, anyway, on this side."

Poirot walked across to it, tried it, then drew back the bolt and tried it again.

"And on the other side as well," he remarked. "Well, that seems to rule out that."

He walked over to the windows, examining each of them in turn.

"And again — nothing. Not even a balcony outside."

"Even if there were," said the inspector impatiently, "I don't see how that would help us, if the maid never left the room."

"Évidemment," said Poirot, not disconcerted. "As Mademoiselle is positive she did not leave the room —"

He was interrupted by the reappearance of the chambermaid and the police searcher.

"Nothing," said the latter laconically.

"I should hope not, indeed," said the chambermaid virtuously. "And that French hussy ought to be ashamed of herself taking away an honest girl's character."

"There, there, my girl; that's all right," said the inspector, opening the door. "Nobody suspects you. You go along and get on with your work."

The chambermaid went unwillingly.

"Going to search her?" she demanded, pointing at Célestine.

"Yes, yes!" He shut the door on her and turned the key.

Célestine accompanied the searcher into the small room in her turn. A few minutes later she also returned. Nothing had been found on her.

The inspector's face grew graver.

"I'm afraid I'll have to ask you to come along with me all the same, miss." He turned to Mrs. Opalsen. "I'm sorry, madam, but all the evidence points that way. If she's not got them on her, they're hidden somewhere about the room."

Célestine uttered a piercing shriek, and clung to Poirot's arm. The latter bent and whispered something in the girl's ear. She looked up at him doubtfully.

"Si, si, mon enfant—I assure you it is better not to resist." Then he turned to the inspector. "You permit, monsieur? A little experiment—purely for my own satisfaction."

"Depends on what it is," replied the police officer noncommittally.

Poirot addressed Célestine once more.

"You have told us that you went into your room to fetch a reel of cotton. Whereabouts was it?"

"On top of the chest of drawers, monsieur."

"And the scissors?"

"They also."

"Would it be troubling you too much, mademoiselle, to ask you to repeat those two actions? You were sitting here with your work, you say?"

Célestine sat down, and then, at a sign from Poirot, rose, passed into the adjoining room, took up an object from the chest of drawers, and returned.

Poirot divided his attention between her movements and a large turnip of a watch which he held in the palm of his hand.

"Again, if you please, mademoiselle."

At the conclusion of the second performance, he made a note in his pocketbook, and returned the watch to his pocket.

"Thank you, mademoiselle. And you, monsieur" — he bowed to the inspector — "for your courtesy."

The inspector seemed somewhat entertained by this excessive politeness. Célestine departed in a flood of tears, accompanied by the woman and the plainclothes official.

Then, with a brief apology to Mrs. Opalsen, the inspector set to work to ransack the room. He pulled out drawers, opened cupboards, completely unmade the bed, and tapped the floor. Mr. Opalsen looked on sceptically.

"You really think you will find them?"

"Yes, sir. It stands to reason. She hadn't time to take them out of the room. The lady's discovering the robbery so soon upset her plans. No, they're here right enough. One of the two must have hidden them — and it's very unlikely for the chambermaid to have done so."

"More than unlikely — impossible!" said Poirot quietly.

"Eh?" The inspector stared.

Poirot smiled modestly.

"I will demonstrate. Hastings, my good friend, take my watch in your hand—with care. It is a family heirloom! Just now I timed Mademoiselle's movements—her first absence from the room was of twelve seconds, her second of fifteen. Now observe my actions. Madame will have the kindness to give me the key of the jewel case. I thank you. My friend Hastings will have the kindness to say 'Go!' "

"Go!" I said.

With almost incredible swiftness, Poirot wrenched open the drawer of the dressing table, extracted the jewel case, fitted the key in the lock, opened the case, selected a piece of jewellery, shut and locked the case, and returned it to the drawer, which he pushed to again. His movements were like lightning.

"Well, mon ami?" he demanded of me breathlessly.

"Forty-six seconds," I replied.

"You see?" He looked round. "There would have not been time for the chambermaid even to take the necklace out, far less hide it."

"Then that settles it on the maid," said the inspector with satisfaction, and returned to his search. He passed into the maid's bedroom next door.

Poirot was frowning thoughtfully. Suddenly he shot a question at Mr. Opalsen.

"This necklace — it was, without doubt, insured?"

Mr. Opalsen looked a trifle surprised at the question.

"Yes," he said hesitatingly, "that is so."

"But what does that matter?" broke in Mrs. Opalsen tearfully. "It's my necklace I want. It was unique. No money could be the same."

"I comprehend, madame," said Poirot soothingly. "I comprehend perfectly. To la femme sentiment is everything — is it not so? But, monsieur, who has not the so fine susceptibility, will doubtless find some slight consolation in the fact."

"Of course, of course," said Mr. Opalsen rather uncertainly. "Still —"

He was interrupted by a shout of triumph from the inspector. He came in dangling something from his fingers.

With a cry, Mrs. Opalsen heaved herself up from her chair. She was a changed woman.

"Oh, oh, my necklace!"

She clasped it to her breast with both hands. We crowded round.

"Where was it?" demanded Opalsen.

"Maid's bed. In among the springs of the wire mattress. She must have stolen it and hidden it there before the chambermaid arrived on the scene."

"You permit, madame?" said Poirot gently. He took the necklace from her and examined it closely; then handed it back with a bow.

"I'm afraid, madame, you'll have to hand it over to us for the time being," said the inspector. "We shall want it for the charge. But it shall be returned to you as soon as possible."

Mr. Opalsen frowned.

"Is that necessary?"

"I'm afraid so, sir. Just a formality."

"Oh, let him take it, Ed!" cired his wife. "I'd feel safer if he did. I shouldn't sleep a wink thinking someone else might try to get hold of it. That wretched girl! And I would never have believed it of her."

"There, there, my dear, don't take on so."

I felt a gentle pressure on my arm. It was Poirot.

"Shall we slip away, my friend? I think our services are no longer needed."

Once outside, however, he hesitated, and then, much to my surprise, he remarked:

"I should rather like to see the room next door."

The door was not locked, and we entered. The room, which was a large double one, was unoccupied. Dust lay about rather noticeably, and my sensitive friend gave a characteristic grimace as he ran his finger round a rectangular mark on a table near the window.

"The service leaves to be desired," he observed dryly.

He was staring thoughtfully out of the window, and seemed to have fallen into a brown study.

"Well?" I demanded impatiently. "What did we come in here for?"

He started.

"Je vous demande pardon, mon ami. I wished to see if the door was really bolted on this side also."

"Well," I said, glancing at the door which communicated with the room we had just left, "it is bolted."

Poirot nodded. He still seemed to be thinking.

"And anyway," I continued, "what does it matter? The case is over. I wish you'd had more chance of distinguishing yourself. But it was the kind of case that even a stiff-backed idiot like that inspector couldn't go wrong over."

Poirot shook his head.

"The case is not over, my friend. It will not be over until we find out who stole the pearls."

"But the maid did!"

"Why do you say that?"

"Why," I stammered, "they were found — actually in her mattress."

"Ta, ta, ta!" said Poirot impatiently. "Those were not the pearls."

"What?"

"Imitation, mon ami."

The statement took my breath away. Poirot was smiling placidly.

"The good inspector obviously knows nothing of jewels. But presently there will be a fine hullabaloo!"

"Come!" I cried, dragging at his arm.

"Where?"

"We must tell the Opalsens at once."

"I think not."

"But that poor woman—"

"Eh bien; that poor woman, as you call her, will have a much better night believing the jewels to be safe."

"But the thief may escape with them!"

"As usual, my friend, you speak without reflection. How do you know that the pearls Mrs. Opalsen locked up so carefully tonight were not the false ones, and that the real robbery did not take place at a much earlier date?"

"Oh!" I said, bewildered.

"Exactly," said Poirot, beaming. "We start again."

He led the way out of the room, paused a moment as though considering, and then walked down to the end of the corridor, stopping outside the small den where the chambermaids and valets of the respective floors congregated. Our particular chambermaid appeared to be holding a small court there, and to be retailing her late experiences to an appreciative audience. She stopped in the middle of a sentence. Poirot bowed with his usual politeness.

"Excuse that I derange you, but I shall be obliged if you will unlock for me the door of Mr. Opalsen's room."

The woman rose willingly, and we accompanied her down the passage again. Mr. Opalsen's room was on the other side of the corridor, its door facing that of his wife's room. The chambermaid unlocked it with her passkey, and we entered.

As she was about to depart Poirot detained her.

"One moment; have you ever seen among the effects of Mr.Opalsen a card like this?"

He held out a plain white card, rather highly glazed and uncommon in appearance. The maid took it and scrutinized it carefully.

"No, sir, I can't say I have. But, anyway, the valet has most to do with the gentlemen's rooms."

"I see. Thank you."

Poirot took back the card. The woman departed. Poirot appeared to reflect a little. Then he gave a short, sharp nod of the head.

"Ring the bell, I pray you, Hastings. Three times for the valet."

I obeyed, devoured with curiosity. Meanwhile Poirot had emptied the wastepaper basket on the floor, and was swiftly going through its contents.

In a few moments the valet answered the bell. To him Poirot put the same question, and handed him the card to examine. But the response was the same. The valet had never seen a card of that particular quality among Mr. Opalsen's belongings. Poirot thanked him, and he withdrew, somewhat unwillingly, with an inquisitive glance at the overturned wastepaper basket and the litter on the floor. He could hardly have helped overhearing Poirot's thoughtful remark as he bundled the torn papers back again:

"And the necklace was heavily insured. . . ."

"Poirot," I cried, "I see—"

"You see nothing, my friend," he replied quickly. "As usual, nothing at all! It is incredible—but there it is. Let us return to our own apartments."

We did so in silence. Once there, to my intense surprise, Poirot effected a rapid change of clothing.

"I go to London tonight," he explained. "It is imperative."

"What?"

"Absolutely. The real work, that of the brain (ah, those brave little grey cells), it is done. I go to seek the confirmation. I shall find it! Impossible to deceive Hercule Poirot!"

"You'll come a cropper one of these days," I observed, rather disgusted by his vanity.

"Do not be enraged, I beg of you, mon ami. I count on you to do me a service—of your friendship."

"Of course," I said eagerly, rather ashamed of my moroseness. "What is it?"

"The sleeve of my coat that I have taken off—will you brush it? See you, a little white powder has clung to it. You without doubt observed me run my finger round the drawer of the dressing table?"

"No, I didn't."

"You should observe my actions, my friend. Thus I obtained the powder on my finger, and, being a little overexcited, I rubbed it on my sleeve; an action without method which I deplore—false to all my principles."

"But what was the powder?" I asked, not particularly interested in Poirot's principles.

"Not the poison of the Borgias," replied Poirot with a twinkle. "I see your imagination mounting. I should say it was French chalk."

"French chalk?"

"Yes, cabinetmakers use it to make drawers run smoothly."

I laughed.

"You old sinner! I thought you were working up to something exciting."

"Au revoir, my friend. I save myself. I fly!"

The door shut behind him. With a smile, half of derision, half of affection, I picked up the coat and stretched out my hand for the clothes brush.

II

The next morning, hearing nothing from Poirot, I went out for a stroll, met some old friends, and lunched with them at their hotel. In the afternoon we went for a spin. A punctured tyre delayed us, and it was past eight when I got back to the Grand Metropolitan.

The first sight that met my eyes was Poirot, looking even more diminutive than usual, sandwiched between the Opalsens, beaming in a state of placid satisfaction.

"Mon ami Hastings!" he cried, and sprang to meet me. "Embrace me, my friend; all has marched to a marvel!"

Luckily, the embrace was merely figurative—not a thing one is always sure of with Poirot.

"Do you mean—" I began.

"Just wonderful, I call it!" said Mrs. Opalsen, smiling all over her fat face. "Didn't I tell you, Ed, that if he couldn't get back my pearls nobody would?"

"You did, my dear, you did. And you were right."

I looked helplessly at Poirot, and he answered the glance.

"My friend Hastings is, as you say in England, all at the seaside. Seat yourself, and I will recount to you all the affair that has so happily ended."

"Ended?"

"But yes. They are arrested."

"Who are arrested?"

"The chambermaid and the valet, parbleu! You did not suspect? Not with my parting hint about the French chalk?"

"You said cabinetmakers used it."

"Certainly they do — to make drawers slide easily. Somebody wanted the drawer to slide in and out without any noise. Who could that be? Obviously, only the chambermaid. The plan was so ingenious that it did not at once leap to the eye — not even to the eye of Hercule Poirot.

"Listen, this was how it was done. The valet was in the empty room next door, waiting. The French maid leaves the room. Quick as a flash the chambermaid whips open the drawer, takes out the jewel case and, slipping back the bolt, passes it through the door. The valet opens it at his leisure with the duplicate key with which he has provided himself, extracts the necklace, and waits his time. Célestine leaves the room again, and — pst! — in a flash the case is passed back again and replaced in the drawer.

"Madame arrives, the theft is discovered. The chambermaid demands to be searched, with a good deal of righteous indignation, and leaves the room without a stain on her character. The imitation necklace with which they have provided themselves has been concealed in the French girl's bed that morning by the chambermaid — a master stroke, ça! "

"But what did you go to London for?"

"You remember the card?"

"Certainly. It puzzled me — and puzzles me still. I thought — "

I hesitated delicately, glancing at Mr. Opalsen.

Poirot laughed heartily.

"Une blague! For the benefit of the valet. The card was one with a specially prepared surface — for fingerprints. I went straight to Scotland Yard, asked for our old friend Inspector Japp, and laid the facts before him. As I had suspected, the fingerprints proved to be those of two well-known jewel thieves who have been 'wanted' for some time. Japp came down with me, the thieves were arrested, and the necklace was discovered in the valet's possession. A clever pair, but they failed in method. Have I not told you, Hastings, at least thirty-six times, that without method —"

"At least thirty-six thousand times!" I interrupted. "But where did their 'method' break down?"

"Mon ami, it is a good plan to take a place as chambermaid or valet — but you must not shirk your work. They left an empty room undusted; and therefore, when the man put down the jewel case on the little table near the communicating door, it left a square mark —"

"I remember," I cried.

"Before, I was undecided. Then — I knew! "

There was a moment's silence.

"And I've got my pearls," said Mrs. Opalsen as a sort of Greek chorus.

"Well," I said, "I'd better have some dinner."

Poirot accompanied me.

"This ought to mean kudos for you," I observed.

Luckily, the embrace was merely figurative—not a thing one is always sure of with Poirot.

"Do you mean—" I began.

"Just wonderful, I call it!" said Mrs. Opalsen, smiling all over her fat face. "Didn't I tell you, Ed, that if he couldn't get back my pearls nobody would?"

"You did, my dear, you did. And you were right."

I looked helplessly at Poirot, and he answered the glance.

"My friend Hastings is, as you say in England, all at the seaside. Seat yourself, and I will recount to you all the affair that has so happily ended."

"Ended?"

"But yes. They are arrested."

"Who are arrested?"

"The chambermaid and the valet, parbleu! You did not suspect? Not with my parting hint about the French chalk?"

"You said cabinetmakers used it."

"Certainly they do—to make drawers slide easily. Somebody wanted the drawer to slide in and out without any noise. Who could that be? Obviously, only the chambermaid. The plan was so ingenious that it did not at once leap to the eye—not even to the eye of Hercule Poirot.

"Listen, this was how it was done. The valet was in the empty room next door, waiting. The French maid leaves the room. Quick as a flash the chambermaid whips open the drawer, takes out the jewel case and, slipping back the bolt, passes it through the door. The valet opens it at his leisure with the duplicate key with which he has provided himself, extracts the necklace, and waits his time. Célestine leaves the room again, and — pst! — in a flash the case is passed back again and replaced in the drawer.

"Madame arrives, the theft is discovered. The chambermaid demands to be searched, with a good deal of righteous indignation, and leaves the room without a stain on her character. The imitation necklace with which they have provided themselves has been concealed in the French girl's bed that morning by the chambermaid — a master stroke, ça! "

"But what did you go to London for?"

"You remember the card?"

"Certainly. It puzzled me — and puzzles me still. I thought — "

I hesitated delicately, glancing at Mr. Opalsen.

Poirot laughed heartily.

"Une blague! For the benefit of the valet. The card was one with a specially prepared surface — for fingerprints. I went straight to Scotland Yard, asked for our old friend Inspector Japp, and laid the facts before him. As I had suspected, the fingerprints proved to be those of two well-known jewel thieves who have been 'wanted' for some time. Japp came down with me, the thieves were arrested, and the necklace was discovered in the valet's possession. A clever pair, but they failed in method. Have I not told you, Hastings, at least thirty-six times, that without method—"

"At least thirty-six thousand times!" I interrupted. "But where did their 'method' break down?"

"Mon ami, it is a good plan to take a place as chambermaid or valet—but you must not shirk your work. They left an empty room undusted; and therefore, when the man put down the jewel case on the little table near the communicating door, it left a square mark—"

"I remember," I cried.

"Before, I was undecided. Then—I knew! "

There was a moment's silence.

"And I've got my pearls," said Mrs. Opalsen as a sort of Greek chorus.

"Well," I said, "I'd better have some dinner."

Poirot accompanied me.

"This ought to mean kudos for you," I observed.

"Pas du tout," replied Poirot tranquilly. "Japp and the local inspector will divide the credit between them. But"—he tapped his pocket—"I have a cheque here, from Mr. Opalsen, and, how you say, my friend? This weekend has not gone according to plan. Shall we return here next weekend—at my expense this time?"

THE ADVENTURE OF THE EGYPTIAN TOMB

I have always considered that one of the most thrilling and dramatic of the many adventures I have shared with Poirot was that of our investigation into the strange series of deaths which followed upon the discovery and opening of the Tomb of King Men-her-Ra.

Hard upon the discovery of the Tomb of Tutankh-Amen by Lord Carnarvon, Sir John Willard and Mr. Bleibner of New York, pursuing their excavations not far from Cairo, in the vicinity of the Pyramids of Gizeh, came unexpectedly on a series of funeral chambers. The greatest interest was aroused by their discovery. The Tomb appeared to be that of King Men-her-Ra, one of those shadowy kings of the Eighth Dynasty, when the Old Kingdom was falling to decay. Little was known about this period, and the discoveries were fully reported in the newspapers.

An event soon occurred which took a profound hold on the public mind. Sir John Willard died quite suddenly of heart failure.

The more sensational newspapers immediately took the opportunity of reviving all the old superstitious stories connected with the ill luck of certain Egyptian treasures. The unlucky Mummy at the British Museum, that hoary old chestnut, was dragged out with fresh zest, was quietly denied by the Museum, but nevertheless enjoyed all its usual vogue.

A fortnight later Mr. Bleibner died of acute blood poisoning, and a few days afterwards a nephew of his shot himself in New York. The "Curse of Men-her-Ra" was the talk of the day, and the magic power of dead-and-gone Egypt was exalted to a fetish point.

It was then that Poirot received a brief note from Lady Willard, widow of the dead archaeologist, asking him to go and see her at her house in Kensington Square. I accompanied him.

Lady Willard was a tall, thin woman, dressed in deep mourning. Her haggard face bore eloquent testimony to her recent grief.

"It is kind of you to have come so promptly, Monsieur Poirot."

"I am at your service, Lady Willard. You wished to consult me?"

"You are, I am aware, a detective, but it is not only as a detective that I wish to consult you. You are a man of original views, I know, you have imagination, experience of the world; tell me, Monsieur Poirot, what are your views on the supernatural?"

Poirot hesitated for a moment before he replied. He seemed to be considering. Finally he said:

"Let us not misunderstand each other, Lady Willard. It is not a general question that you are asking me there. It has a personal application, has it not? You are referring obliquely to the death of your late husband?"

"That is so," she admitted.

"You want me to investigate the circumstances of his death?"

"I want you to ascertain for me exactly how much is newspaper chatter, and how much may be said to be founded on fact? Three deaths, Monsieur Poirot — each one explicable taken by itself, but taken together surely an almost unbelievable coincidence, and all within a month of the opening of the tomb! It may be mere superstition, it may be some potent curse from the past that operates in ways undreamed of by modern science. The fact remains—three deaths! And I am afraid, Monsieur Poirot, horribly afraid. It may not yet be the end."

"For whom do you fear?"

"For my son. When the news of my husband's death came I was ill. My son, who has just come down from Oxford, went out there. He brought the—the body home, but now he has gone out again, in spite of my prayers and entreaties. He is so fascinated by the work that he intends to take his father's place and carry on the system of excavations. You may think me a foolish, credulous woman, but, Monsieur Poirot, I am afraid. Supposing that the spirit of the dead King is not yet appeased? Perhaps to you I seem to be talking nonsense—"

"No, indeed, Lady Willard," said Poirot quickly. "I, too, believe in the force of superstition, one of the greatest forces the world has ever known."

I looked at him in surprise. I should never have credited Poirot with being superstitious. But the little man was obviously in earnest.

"What you really demand is that I shall protect your son? I will do my utmost to keep him from harm."

"Yes, in the ordinary way, but against an occult influence?"

"In volumes of the Middle Ages, Lady Willard, you will find many ways of counteracting black magic. Perhaps they knew more than we moderns with all our boasted science. Now let us come to facts, that I may have guidance. Your husband had always been a devoted Egyptologist, hadn't he?"

"Yes, from his youth upwards. He was one of the greatest living authorities upon the subject."

"But Mr. Bleibner, I understand, was more or less of an amateur?"

"Oh, quite. He was a very wealthy man who dabbled freely in any subject that happened to take his fancy. My husband managed to interest him in Egyptology, and it was his money that was so useful in financing the expedition."

"And the nephew? What do you know of his tastes? Was he with the party at all?"

"I do not think so. In fact I never knew of his existence till I read of his death in the paper. I do not think he and Mr. Bleibner can have been at all intimate. He never spoke of having any relations."

"Who are the other members of the party?"

"Well, there's Dr. Tosswill, a minor official connected with the British Museum; Mr. Schneider of the Metropolitan Museum in New York; a young American secretary; Dr. Ames, who accompanies the expedition in his professional capacity; and Hassan, my husband's devoted native servant."

"Do you remember the name of the American secretary?"

"Harper, I think, but I cannot be sure. He had not been with Mr. Bleibner very long, I know. He was a very pleasant young fellow."

"Thank you, Lady Willard."

"If there is anything else—"

"For the moment, nothing. Leave it now in my hands, and be assured that I will do all that is humanly possible to protect your son."

They were not exactly reassuring words, and I observed Lady Willard wince as he uttered them. Yet, at the same time, the fact that he had not pooh-poohed her fears seemed in itself to be a relief to her.

For my part I had never before suspected that Poirot had so deep a vein of superstition in his nature. I tackled him on the subject as we went homewards. His manner was grave and earnest.

"But yes, Hastings. I believe in these things. You must not underrate the force of superstition."

"What are we going to do about it?"

"Toujours pratique, the good Hastings! Eh bien, to begin with we are going to cable to New York for fuller details of young Mr. Bleibner's death."

He duly sent off his cable. The reply was full and precise. Young Rupert Bleibner had been in low water for several years. He had been a beachcomber and a remittance man in several South Sea islands, but had returned to New York two years ago, where he had rapidly sunk lower and lower. The most significant thing, to my mind, was that he had recently managed to borrow enough money to take him to Egypt. "I've a good friend there I can borrow from," he had declared. Here, however, his plans had gone awry. He had returned to New York cursing his skinflint of an uncle who cared more for the bones of dead and gone kings than his own flesh and blood. It was during his sojourn in Egypt that the death of Sir John Willard had occurred. Rupert had plunged once more into his life of dissipation in New York, and then, without warning, he had committed suicide, leaving behind him a letter which contained some curious phrases. It seemed written in a sudden fit of remorse. He referred to himself as a leper and an outcast, and the letter ended by declaring that such as he were better dead.

A shadowy theory leapt into my brain. I had never really believed in the vengeance of a long dead Egyptian king. I saw here a more modern crime. Supposing this young man had decided to do away with his uncle — preferably by poison. By mistake, Sir John Willard receives the fatal dose. The young man returns to New York, haunted by his crime. The news of his uncle's death reaches him. He realizes how unnecessary his crime has been, and stricken with remorse takes his own life.

I outlined my solution to Poirot. He was interested.

"It is ingenious what you have thought of there — decidedly it is ingenious. It may even be true. But you leave out of count the fatal influence of the Tomb."

I shrugged my shoulders.

"You still think that has something to do with it?"

"So much so, mon ami, that we start for Egypt tomorrow."

"What?" I cried, astonished.

"I have said it." An expression of conscious heroism spread over Poirot's face. Then he groaned. "But oh," he lamented, "the sea! The hateful sea!"

It was a week later. Beneath our feet was the golden sand of the desert. The hot sun poured down overhead. Poirot, the picture of misery, wilted by my side. The little man was not a good traveller. Our four days' voyage from Marseilles had been one long agony to him. He had landed at Alexandria the wraith of his former self, even his usual neatness had deserted him. We had arrived in Cairo and had driven out at once to the Mena House Hotel, right in the shadow of the Pyramids.

The charm of Egypt had laid hold of me. Not so Poirot. Dressed precisely the same as in London, he carried a small clothes brush in his pocket and waged an unceasing war on the dust which accumulated on his dark apparel.

"And my boots," he wailed. "Regard them, Hastings. My boots, of the neat patent leather, usually so smart and shining. See, the sand is inside them, which is painful, and outside them, which outrages the eyesight. Also the heat, it causes my moustaches to become limp—but limp!"

"Look at the Sphinx," I urged. "Even I can feel the mystery and the charm it exhales."

Poirot looked at it discontentedly.

"It has not the air happy," he declared. "How could it, half-buried in sand in that untidy fashion. Ah, this cursed sand!"

"Come, now, there's a lot of sand in Belgium," I reminded him, mindful of a holiday spent at Knocke-sur-mer in the midst of "Les dunes impeccables" as the guidebook had phrased it.

"Not in Brussels," declared Poirot. He gazed at the Pyramids thoughtfully. "It is true that they, at least, are of a shape solid and geometrical, but their surface is of an unevenness most unpleasing. And the palm trees I like them not. Not even do they plant them in rows!"

I cut short his lamentations, by suggesting that we should start for the camp. We were to ride there on camels, and the beasts were patiently kneeling, waiting for us to mount, in charge of several picturesque boys headed by a voluble dragoman.

I pass over the spectacle of Poirot on a camel. He started by groans and lamentations and ended by shrieks, gesticulations and invocations to the Virgin Mary and every Saint in the calendar. In the end, he descended ignominiously and finished the journey on a diminutive donkey. I must admit that a trotting camel is no joke for the amateur. I was stiff for several days.

At last we neared the scene of the excavations. A sunburnt man with a grey beard, in white clothes and wearing a helmet, came to meet us.

"Monsieur Poirot and Captain Hastings? We received your cable. I'm sorry that there was no one to meet you in Cairo. An unforeseen event occurred which completely disorganized our plans."

Poirot paled. His hand, which had stolen to his clothes brush, stayed its course.

"Not another death?" he breathed.

"Yes."

"Sir Guy Willard?" I cried.

"No, Captain Hastings. My American colleague, Mr. Schneider."

"And the cause?" demanded Poirot.

"Tetanus."

I blanched. All around me I seemed to feel an atmosphere of evil, subtle and menacing. A horrible thought flashed across me. Supposing I were next?

"Mon Dieu," said Poirot, in a very low voice, "I do not understand this. It is horrible. Tell me, monsieur, there is no doubt that it was tetanus?"

"I believe not. But Dr. Ames will tell you more than I can do."

"Ah, of course, you are not the doctor."

"My name is Tosswill."

This, then, was the British expert described by Lady Willard as being a minor official at the British Museum. There was something at once grave and steadfast about him that took my fancy.

"If you will come with me," continued Dr. Tosswill. "I will take you to Sir Guy Willard. He was most anxious to be informed as soon as you should arrive."

We were taken across the camp to a large tent. Dr. Tosswill lifted up the flap and we entered. Three men were sitting inside.

"Monsieur Poirot and Captain Hastings have arrived, Sir Guy," said Tosswill.

The youngest of the three men jumped up and came forward to greet us. There was a certain impulsiveness in his manner which reminded me of his mother. He was not nearly so sunburnt as the others, and that fact, coupled with a certain haggardness round the eyes, made him look older than his twenty-two years. He was clearly endeavouring to bear up under a severe mental strain.

He introduced his two companions, Dr. Ames, a capable-looking man of thirty-odd, with a touch of greying hair at the temples, and Mr. Harper, the secretary, a pleasant lean young man wearing the national insignia of horn-rimmed spectacles.

After a few minutes' desultory conversation the latter went out, and Dr. Tosswill followed him. We were left alone with Sir Guy and Dr. Ames.

"Please ask any questions you want to ask, Monsieur Poirot," said Willard. "We are utterly dumbfounded at this strange series of disasters, but it isn't — it can't be, anything but coincidence."

There was a nervousness about his manner which rather belied the words. I saw that Poirot was studying him keenly.

"Your heart is really in this work, Sir Guy?"

"Rather. No matter what happens, or what comes of it, the work is going on. Make up your mind to that."

Poirot wheeled round on the other.

"What have you to say to that, monsieur le docteur?"

"Well," drawled the doctor, "I'm not for quitting myself."

Poirot made one of those expressive grimaces of his.

"Then, évidemment, we must find out just how we stand. When did Mr. Schneider's death take place?"

"Three days ago."

"You are sure it was tetanus?"

"Dead sure."

"It couldn't have been a case of strychnine poisoning, for instance?"

"No, Monsieur Poirot, I see what you are getting at. But it was a clear case of tetanus."

"Did you not inject antiserum?"

"Certainly we did," said the doctor dryly. "Every conceivable thing that could be done was tried."

"Had you the antiserum with you?"

"No. We procured it from Cairo."

"Have there been any other cases of tetanus in the camp?"

"No, not one."

"Are you certain that the death of Mr. Bleibner was not due to tetanus?"

"Absolutely plumb certain. He had a scratch upon his thumb which became poisoned, and septicaemia set in. It sounds pretty much the same to a layman, I dare say, but the two things are entirely different."

"Then we have four deaths—all totally dissimilar, one heart failure, one blood poisoning, one suicide and one tetanus."

"Exactly, Monsieur Poirot."

"Are you certain that there is nothing which might link the four together?"

"I don't quite understand you?"

"I will put it plainly. Was any act committed by those four men which might seem to denote disrespect to the spirit of Men-her-Ra?"

The doctor gazed at Poirot in astonishment.

"You're talking through your hat, Monsieur Poirot. Surely you've not been guyed into believing all that fool talk?"

"Absolute nonsense," muttered Willard angrily.

Poirot remained placidly immovable, blinking a little out of his green cat's eyes.

THE KIDNAPPED PRIME MINISTER

I.

NOW that war and the problems of war are things of the past, I think I may safely venture to reveal to the world the part which my friend Poirot played in a moment of national crisis. The secret has been well guarded. Not a whisper of it reached the Press. But now that the need for secrecy has gone by, I feel it is only just that England should know the debt it owes to my quaint little friend, whose marvellous brain so ably averted a great catastrophe.

One evening after dinner — I will not particularise the date; it suffices to say that it was at the time when "Peace by negotiation" was the parrot-cry of England's enemies — my friend and I were sitting in his rooms. After being invalided out of the Army I had been given a recruiting job, and it had become my custom to drop in on Poirot in the evenings after dinner and talk with him of any cases of interest that he might have on hand.

I was attempting to discuss with him the sensational news of that day — no less than an attempted assassination of Mr. David MacAdam, England's Prime Minister. The account in the papers had evidently been carefully censored. No details were given, save that the Prime Minister had had a marvellous escape, the bullet just grazing his cheek.
I considered that our police must have been shamefully careless for such an outrage to be possible. I could well understand that the German agents in England would be willing to risk much for such an achievement. "Fighting Mac," as his own party had nicknamed him, had strenuously and unequivocally combated the Pacifist influence which was becoming so prevalent.

He was more than England's Prime Minister—he was England; and to have removed him from his sphere of influence would have been a crushing and paralysing blow to Britain.

Poirot was busy mopping a grey suit with a minute sponge. Never was there a dandy such as Hercule Poirot. Neatness and order were his passion. Now, with the odour of benzine filling the air, he was quite unable to give me his full attention. "In a little minute I am with you, my friend. I have all but finished. The spot of grease—he is not good—I remove him—so!" He waved his sponge.

I smiled as I lit another cigarette.

"Anything interesting on?" I inquired, after a minute or two. "I assist a—how do you call it?—charlady to find her husband. A difficult affair, needing the tact. For I have a little idea that when he is found he will not be pleased. What would you? For my part, I sympathise with him. He was a man of discrimination to lose himself."

I laughed.

"At last! The spot of grease, he is gone! I am at your disposal." "I was asking you what you thought of this attempt to assassinate MacAdam?"

"Enfantillage!" replied Poirot promptly. "One can hardly take it seriously. To fire with the rifle—never does it succeed. It is a device of the past."

"It was very near succeeding this time," I reminded him. Poirot shook his head impatiently. He was about to reply when the landlady thrust her head round the door and informed him that there were two gentlemen below who wanted to see him.

"They won't give their names, Sir, but they says as it's very important."

"Let them mount," said Poirot, carefully folding his grey trousers.

In a few minutes the two visitors were ushered in, and my heart gave a leap as in the foremost I recognised no less a personage than Lord Estair, Leader of the House of Commons; whilst his companion, Mr. Bernard Dodge, was also a member of the War Cabinet, and, as I knew, a close personal friend of the Prime Minister.

"M. Poirot?" said Lord Estair interrogatively. My friend bowed. The great man looked at me and hesitated. "My business is private."

"You may speak freely before Captain Hastings," said my friend, nodding to me to remain. "He has not all the gifts, no! But I answer for his discretion."

Lord Estair still hesitated, but Mr. Dodge broke in abruptly. "Oh, come on—don't let's beat about the bush! As far as I can see, the whole of England will know the hole we're in soon enough. Time's everything."

"Pray be seated, Messieurs," said Poirot politely. "Will you take the big chair, milor?"

Lord Estair started slightly. "You know me?"

Poirot smiled. "Certainly. I read the little papers with the pictures. How should I not know you?"

"M. Poirot, I have come to consult you upon a matter of the most vital urgency. I must ask for absolute secrecy."

"You have the word of Hercule Poirot—I can say no more!" said my friend grandiloquently.

"It concerns the Prime Minister. We are in grave trouble."
"We're up a tree!" interposed Mr. Dodge.

"The injury is serious, then?" I asked.

"What injury?"

"The bullet wound."

"Oh, that!" cried Mr. Dodge contemptuously. "That's old history."

"As my colleague says," continued Lord Estair, "that affair is over and done with. Luckily, it failed. I wish I could say as much for the second attempt."

"There has been a second attempt, then?"

"Yes, though not of the same nature. M. Poirot, the Prime Minister has disappeared."

"What?"

"He has been kidnapped!"

"Impossible!" I cried, stupefied. Poirot threw a withering glance at me, which I knew enjoined me to keep my mouth shut.

"Unfortunately, impossible as it seems, it is only too true," continued his Lordship.

Poirot looked at Mr. Dodge. "You said just now, Monsieur, that time was everything. What did you mean by that?"

The two men exchanged glances, and then Lord Estair said, "You have heard, M. Poirot, of the approaching Allied Conference?"

My friend nodded.

"For obvious reasons, no details have been given of when and where it is to take place. But, although it has been kept out of the newspapers, the date is, of course, widely known in diplomatic circles. The Conference is to be held to-morrow — Thursday — evening at Versailles. Now you perceive the terrible gravity of the situation. I will not conceal from you that the Prime Minister's presence at the Conference is a vital necessity. The Pacifist propaganda, started and maintained by the German agents in our midst, has been very active. It is the universal opinion that the turning point of the Conference will be the strong personality of the Prime Minister. His absence may have the most serious results — possibly a premature and disastrous peace. And we have no one who can be sent in his place. He alone can represent England."

Poirot's face bad grown very grave. "Then you regard the kidnapping of the Prime Minister as a direct attempt to prevent his being present at the Conference?"

"Most certainly I do. He was actually on his way to France at the time."

"And the Conference is to be held?"

"At nine o'clock to-morrow night."

Poirot drew an enormous watch from his pocket. "It is now a quarter to nine."

"Twenty-four hours," said Mr. Dodge thoughtfully.

"And a quarter," amended Poirot. "Do not forget the quarter, Monsieur—it may come in useful. Now for the details—the abduction, did it take place in England or in France?"

"In France. Mr. MacAdam crossed to France this morning. He was to stay to-night as the guest of the Commander-in-Chief, proceeding to-morrow to Paris. He was conveyed across the Channel by destroyer. At Boulogne he was met by a car from General Headquarters and one of the Commander-in-Chief's A.D.C.s."

"Eh bien?"

"Well, they started from Boulogne—but they never arrived."

"What?"

"M. Poirot, it was a bogus car and a bogus A.D.C. The real car was found in a side road, with the chauffeur and the A.D.C. neatly gagged and bound."

"And the bogus car?"

"Is still at large."

Poirot made a gesture of impatience. "Incredible! Surely it cannot escape attention for long?"

"So we thought. It seemed merely a question of searching thoroughly. That part of France is under Military Law. We were convinced that the car could not go long unnoticed. The French police, our own Scotland Yard men, and the Military are straining every nerve. It is, as you say, incredible—but nothing has been discovered!"

At that moment a tap came at the door, and a young officer entered with a heavily sealed envelope which he handed to Lord Estair.

"Just through from France, Sir. I brought it on here, as you directed."

The Minister tore it open eagerly, and uttered an exclamation. The officer withdrew.

"Here is news at last! This telegram has just been decoded. They have found the second car, also the secretary, Daniels, chloroformed, gagged, and bound, in an abandoned farm near C— —. He remembers nothing, except something being pressed against his mouth and nose from behind, and struggling to free himself. The police are satisfied as to the genuineness of his statement."

"And they have found nothing else?"

"No."

"Not the Prime Minister's dead body? Then there is hope. But it is strange. Why, after trying to shoot him this morning, are they now taking so much trouble to keep him alive?"
Dodge shook his head. "One thing's quite certain. They're determined at all costs to prevent his attending the Conference."

"If it is humanly possible, the Prime Minister shall be there. God grant it is not too late. Now, Messieurs, recount to me everything—from the beginning. I must know about this shooting affair as well."

"Last night, the Prime Minister, accompanied by one of his secretaries, Captain Daniels— —"

"The same who accompanied him to France?"

"Yes. As I was saying, they motored down to Windsor, where the Prime Minister was granted an Audience. Early this morning, he returned to town, and it was on the way that the attempted assassination took place."

"One moment, if you please. Who is this Captain Daniels? You have his dossier?"

Lord Estair smiled. "I thought you would ask me that. We do not know very much of him. He is of no particular family. He has served in the English Army, and is an extremely able secretary, being an exceptionally fine linguist. I believe he speaks seven languages. It is for that reason that the Prime Minister chose him to accompany him to France."

"Has he any relatives in England."

"Two aunts. A Mrs. Everard, who lives at Hampstead, and a Miss Daniels, who lives near Ascot."

"Ascot? That is near to Windsor, is it not?"

"That point has not been overlooked. But it has led to nothing."

"You regard the Capitaine Daniels, then, as above suspicion?"

A shade of bitterness crept into Lord Estair's voice, as he replied: "No, M. Poirot. In these days, I should hesitate before I pronounced anyone above suspicion."

"Très bien. Now I understand, milor, that the Prime Minister would, as a matter of course, be under vigilant police protection, which ought to render any assault upon him an impossibility?"

Lord Estair bowed his head. "That is so. The Prime Minister's car was closely followed by another car containing detectives in plain clothes. Mr. MacAdam knew nothing of these precautions. He is personally a most fearless man, and would be inclined to sweep them away arbitrarily. But, naturally, the police make their own arrangements. In fact, the Premier's chauffeur, O'Murphy, is a C.I.D. man."

"O'Murphy? That is a name of Ireland, is it not so?"

"Yes, he is an Irishman."

"From what part of Ireland?"

"County Clare, I believe."

"Tiens! But proceed, Milor."

"The Premier started for London. The car was a closed one. He and Captain Daniels sat inside. The second car followed as usual. But, unluckily, for some unknown reason, the Prime Minister's car deviated from the main road — —"

"At a point where the road curves?" interrupted Poirot. "Yes — but how did you know?"

"Oh! C'est évident! Continue!"

"For some unknown reason," continued Lord Estair, "the Premier's car left the main road. The police car, unaware of the deviation, continued to keep to the high road. At a short distance down the unfrequented lane, the Prime Minister's car was suddenly held up by a band of masked men. The chauffeur — —"

"That brave O'Murphy!" murmured Poirot thoughtfully. "The chauffeur, momentarily taken aback, jammed on the brakes. The Prime Minister put his head out of the window. Instantly a shot rang out — then another. The first one grazed his cheek, the second, fortunately, went wide. The chauffeur, now realising the danger, instantly forged straight ahead, scattering the band of men."

"A near escape," I ejaculated, with a shiver.

"Mr. MacAdam refused to make any fuss over the slight wound he had received. He declared it was only a scratch. He stopped at a local cottage hospital, where it was dressed and bound up — he did not, of course reveal his identity. He then drove, as per schedule, straight to Charing Cross, where a special train for Dover was awaiting him, and after a brief account of what had happened had been given to the anxious police by Captain Daniels, he duly departed for France. At Dover, he went on board the waiting destroyer. At Boulogne, as you know, the bogus car was waiting for him, carrying the Union Jack, and correct in every detail."

"That is all you have to tell me?"
"Yes."

"There is no other circumstance that you have omitted, milor?"
"Well, there is one rather peculiar thing."

"Yes?"

"The Prime Minister's car did not return home after leaving the Prime Minister at Charing Cross. The police were anxious to interview O'Murphy, so a search was instituted at once. The car was discovered standing outside a certain unsavoury little restaurant in Soho, which is well known as a meeting-place of German agents."

"And the chauffeur?"

"The chauffeur was nowhere to be found. He, too, had disappeared."

"So," said Poirot thoughtfully. "There are two disappearances: the Prime Minister in France, and O'Murphy in London." He looked keenly at Lord Estair, who made a gesture of despair.

"I can only tell you, M. Poirot, that if anyone had suggested to me yesterday that O'Murphy was a traitor, I should have laughed in his face."

"And to-day?"

"To-day I do not know what to think."

Poirot nodded gravely. He looked at his turnip of a watch again.

"I understand that I have carte blanche, Messieurs — in every way, I mean? I must be able to go where I choose, and how I choose."

"Perfectly. There is a special train leaving for Dover in an hour's time, with a further contingent from Scotland Yard. You shall be accompanied by a Military officer and a C.I.D. man, who will hold themselves at your disposal in every way. Is that satisfactory?"

"Quite. One more question before you leave, Messieurs. What made you come to me? I am unknown, obscure, in this great London of yours."

"We sought you out on the express recommendation and wish of a very great man of your own country."

"Comment? My old friend the Préfet — ?"

Lord Estair shook his head.

"One higher than the Préfet. One whose word was once law in Belgium — and shall be again! That England has sworn!"

Poirot's hand flew swiftly to a dramatic salute. "Amen to that! Ah! but my Master does not forget....Messieurs, I, Hercule Poirot, will serve you faithfully. Heaven only send that it will be in time. But this is dark — dark....I cannot see."

II.

"Well, Poirot," I cried impatiently, as the door closed behind the Ministers. "What do you think?"

My friend was busy packing a minute suit-case, with quick, deft movements. He shook his head thoughtfully. "I do not know what to think. My brains desert me."

"Why, as you said, kidnap him, when a knock on the head would do as well?" I mused.

"Pardon me, mon ami, but I didnot quite say that. It is undoubtedly far more their affair to kidnap him."

"But why?"

"Because uncertainty creates panic. That is one reason. Were the Prime Minister dead, it would be a terrible calamity, but the situation would have to be faced. But now you have paralysis. Will the Prime Minister reappear, or will he not? Is he dead or alive? Nobody knows, and until they know, nothing definite can be done. And, as I tell you, uncertainty breeds panic, which is what les Boches are playing for. Then, again, if the kidnappers are holding him secretly somewhere, they have the advantage of being able to make terms with both sides. The German Government is not a liberal paymaster, as a rule, but no doubt they can be made to disgorge substantial remittances in such a case as this. Thirdly, they run no risk of the hangman's rope. Oh, decidedly, kidnapping is their affair."

"Then, if that is so, why should they first try to shoot him?" Poirot made a gesture of anger. "Ah! that is just what I do not understand! It is inexplicable — stupid! They have all their arrangements made (and very good arrangements, too!) for the abduction, and yet they imperil the whole affair by a melodramatic attack, worthy of a cinema, and quite as unreal. It is almost impossible to believe in it, with its band of masked men, not twenty miles from London!"

"Perhaps they were two quite separate attempts which happened irrespective of each other," I suggested.
"Ah, no, that would be too much of a coincidence! Then, further — who is the traitor? There must have been a traitor — in the first affair, anyway. But who was it — Daniels or O'Murphy? It must have been one of the two, or why did the car leave the main road? We cannot suppose that the Prime Minister connived at his own assassination! Did O'Murphy take that turning of his own accord, or was it Daniels who told him to do so?"

"Surely it must have been O'Murphy's doing."

"Yes, because if it was Daniels, the Prime Minister would have heard the order, and would have asked the reason. But there are altogether too many 'whys' in this affair, and they contradict each other. If O'Murphy is an honest man, why did he leave the main road? But if he was a dishonest man, why did he start the car again when only two shots had been fired—thereby, in all probability, saving the Prime Minister's life? And, again, if he was honest, why did he, immediately on leaving Charing Cross, drive to a well-known rendezvous of German spies?"

"It looks bad," I said.

"Let us look at the case with method. What have we for and against these two men? Take O'Murphy first. Against: That his conduct in leaving the main road was suspicious; that he is an Irishman from County Clare; that he has disappeared in a highly suggestive manner. For: That his promptness in re-starting the car saved the Premier's life; that he is a Scotland Yard man, and, obviously, from the post allotted to him, a trusted detective. Now for Daniels. There is not much against him, except the fact that nothing is known of his antecedents, and that he speaks too many languages for a good Englishman! (Pardon me, mon ami, but, as linguists, you are deplorable!) Now for him, we have the fact that he was found gagged, bound, and chloroformed—which does not look as though he had anything to do with the matter."

"He might have gagged and bound himself, to divert suspicion."

Poirot shook his head. "The French police would make no mistake of that kind. Besides, once he had attained his object, and the Prime Minister was safely abducted, there would not be much point in his remaining behind. His accomplices could have gagged and chloroformed him, of course, but I fail to see what object they hoped to accomplish by it. He can be of little use to them now, for, until the circumstances concerning the Prime Minister have been cleared up, he is bound to be closely watched."

"Perhaps he hoped to start the police on a false scent?"

"Then why did he not do so? He merely says that something was pressed over his nose and mouth, and that he remembers nothing more. There is no false scent there. It sounds remarkably like the truth."

"Well," I said, glancing at the clock, "I suppose we'd better start for the station. You may find more clues in France." "Possibly, mon ami, but I doubt it. It is still incredible to me that the Prime Minister has not been discovered in that limited area, where the difficulty of concealing him must be tremendous. If the military and the police of two countries have not found him, how shall I?"

At Charing Cross we were met by Mr. Dodge.

"This is Detective Barnes, of Scotland Yard, and Major Norman. They will hold themselves entirely at your disposal. Good luck to you. It's a bad business, but I've not given up hope. Must be off now." And the Minister strode rapidly away.

We chatted in a desultory fashion with Major Norman. In the centre of the little group of men on the platform I recognised a little ferret-faced fellow talking to a tall, fair man. He was an old acquaintance of Poirot's — Detective-Inspector Japp, supposed to be one of the smartest of Scotland Yard's officers. He came over and greeted my friend cheerfully.

"I heard you were on this job too. Smart bit of work. So far they've got away with the goods all right. But I can't believe they can keep him hidden long. Our people are going through France with a toothcomb. So are the French. I can't help feeling it's only a matter of hours now."

"That is, if he's still alive," remarked the tall detective gloomily.

Japp's face fell. "Yes....But somehow I've got the feeling he's alive all right."

Poirot nodded. "Yes, yes; he's alive. But can he be found in time? I, like you, did not believe he could be hidden so long." The whistle blew, and we all trooped up into the Pullman car. Then, with a slow, unwilling jerk, the train drew out of the station.

It was a curious journey. The Scotland Yard men crowded together. Maps of Northern France were spread out, and eager forefingers traced the lines of roads and villages. Each man had his own pet theory. Poirot showed none of his usual loquacity, but sat staring in front of him, with an expression on his face that reminded me of a puzzled child. I talked to Norman, whom I found quite an amusing fellow. On arriving at Dover Poirot's behaviour moved me to intense amusement. The little man, as he went on board the boat, clutched desperately at my arm. The wind was blowing lustily.

"Mon Dieu!" he murmured. "This is terrible!"

"Have courage, Poirot," I cried. "You will succeed. You will find him. I am sure of it."

"Ah, mon ami, you mistake my emotion. It is this villainous sea that troubles me! The mal de mer— it is horrible suffering!"

"Oh!" I said, rather taken aback.

The first throb of the engines was felt, and Poirot groaned and closed his eyes.

"Major Norman has a map of Northern France if you would like to study it?"

Poirot shook his head impatiently.

"But no—but no! Leave me, my friend. See you, to think, the stomach and the brain must be in harmony. Laverguier has a method most excellent for averting the mal de mer. You breathe in—and out—slowly, so—turning the head from left to right and counting six between each breath."

I left him to his gymnastic endeavours, and went on deck. As we came slowly into Boulogne Harbour Poirot appeared, neat and smiling, and announced to me in a whisper that "Laverguier's system had succeeded to a marvel!"

Japp's forefinger was still tracing imaginary routes on his map. "Nonsense! The car started from Boulogne—here they branched off. Now, my idea is that they transferred the Prime Minister to another car. See?"

"Well," said the tall detective, "I shall make for the seaports. Ten to one, they've smuggled him on board a ship."

Japp shook his head. "Too obvious. The order went out at once to close all the ports."

The day was just breaking as we landed. Major Norman touched Poirot on the arm. "There's a military car here waiting for you, Sir."

"Thank you, Monsieur. But, for the moment, I do not propose to leave Boulogne."

"What?"

"No, we will enter this hotel here, by the quay."

He suited the action to the word, demanded and was accorded a private room. We three followed him, puzzled and uncomprehending.

He shot a quick glance at us. "It is not so that the good detective should act, eh? I perceive your thought. He must be full of energy. He must rush to and fro. He should prostrate himself on the dusty road and seek the marks of tyres through a little glass. He must gather up the cigarette-end, the fallen match? That is your idea, is it not?"

His eyes challenged us. "But I—Hercule Poirot—tell you that it is not so! The true clues are within—here!" He tapped his forehead. "See you, I need not have left London. It would have been sufficient for me to sit quietly in my rooms there. All that matters is the little grey cells within. Secretly and silently they do their part, until suddenly I call for a map, and I lay my finger on a spot—so—and I say: the Prime Minister is there! And it is so! With method and logic one can accomplish anything! This frantic rushing to France was a mistake—it is playing a child's game of hide-and-seek. But now, though it may be too late, I will set to work the right way, from within. Silence, my friends, I beg of you."

And for five long hours the little man sat motionless, blinking his eyelids like a cat, his green eyes flickering and becoming steadily greener and greener. The Scotland Yard man was obviously contemptuous, Major Norman was bored and impatient, and I myself found the time pass with wearisome slowness.

Finally, I got up, and strolled as noiselessly as I could to the window. The matter was becoming a farce. I was secretly concerned for my friend. If he failed, I would have preferred him to fail in a less ridiculous manner. Out of the window I idly watched the daily leave boat, belching forth columns of smoke, as she lay alongside the quay.

Suddenly I was aroused by Poirot's voice close to my elbow. "Mes amis, let us start!"

I turned. An extraordinary transformation had come over my friend. His eyes were flickering with excitement, his chest was swelled to the uttermost.

"I have been an imbecile, my friends! But I see daylight at last."

Major Norman moved hastily to the door. "I'll order the car." "There is no need. I shall not use it. Thank heaven the wind has fallen."

"Do you mean you are going to walk, Sir?"

"No, my young friend. I am no St. Peter. I prefer to cross the sea by boat."

"To cross the sea?"

"Yes. To work with method, one must begin from the beginning. And the beginning of this affair was in England. Therefore, we return to England."

III.

At three o'clock, we stood once more upon Charing Cross platform. To all our expostulations, Poirot turned a deaf ear, and reiterated again and again that to start at the beginning was not a waste of time, but the only way. On the way over, he had conferred with Norman in a low voice, and the latter had despatched a sheaf of telegrams from Dover.
Owing to the special passes held by Norman, we got through everywhere in record time. In London, a large police car was waiting for us, with some plain-clothes men, one of whom handed a typewritten sheet of paper to my friend. He answered my inquiring glance.

"A list of the cottage hospitals within a certain radius west of London. I wired for it from Dover."

We were whirled rapidly through the London streets. On we went, through Shepherd's Bush, Ealing, Hanwell. I began to see our objective. We were on the Windsor Road. Through Windsor, and on to Ascot. My heart gave a leap. Ascot was where Daniels had an aunt living. We were after him, then, not O'Murphy.

We duly stopped at the gate of a trim villa. Poirot jumped out and rang the bell. I saw a perplexed frown dimming the radiance of his face. Plainly, he was not satisfied. The bell was answered. He was ushered inside. In a few moments he reappeared, and climbed into the car with a short, sharp shake of his head. My hopes began to die down. It was past four now. Even if he found certain evidence incriminating Daniels, what would be the good of it, unless he could wring from someone the exact spot in France where they were holding the Prime Minister?

Our return progress towards London was an interrupted one. We deviated from the main road more than once, and occasionally stopped at a small building, which I had no difficulty in recognising as a cottage hospital. Poirot only spent a few minutes at each, but at every halt his radiant assurance was more and more restored.

He whispered something to Norman, to which the latter replied:

"Yes, if you turn off to the left, you will find them waiting by the bridge."

We turned up a side road, and in the failing light, I discerned a second car, waiting by the side of the road. It contained two men in plain clothes. Poirot got down and spoke to them, and then we started off in a northerly direction, the other car following close behind.

We drove for some time, our objective being obviously one of the northern suburbs of London. Finally, we drove up to the front door of a tall house, standing a little back from the road in its own grounds.

Norman and I were left with the car. Poirot and one of the detectives went up to the door and rang. A neat parlourmaid opened it. The detective spoke.

"I am a police officer, and I have a warrant to search this house."

The girl gave a little scream, and a tall, handsome woman of middle age appeared behind her in the hall.

"Shut the door, Edith. They are burglars, I expect."
But Poirot swiftly inserted his foot in the door, and at the same moment blew a whistle. Instantly the other detectives ran up, and poured into the house, shutting the door behind them.

Norman and I spent about five minutes cursing our forced inactivity. Finally the door reopened, and the men emerged, escorting three prisoners—a woman and two men. The woman, and one of the men, were taken to the second car. The other man was placed in our car by Poirot himself.
"I must go with the others, my friend. But have great care of this gentleman. You do not know him, no? Eh bien, let me present to you, M. O'Murphy!"

O'Murphy! I gaped at him open-mouthed as we started again. He was not handcuffed, but I did not fancy he would try to escape. He sat there staring in front of him as though dazed. Anyway, Norman and I would be more than a match for him. To my surprise, we still kept a northerly route. We were not returning to London, then! I was much puzzled. Suddenly, as the car slowed down, I recognised that we were close to Hendon Aerodrome. Immediately I grasped Poirot's idea. He proposed to reach France by aeroplane.

It was a sporting idea, but on the face of it, impracticable. A telegram would be far quicker. Time was everything. He must leave the personal glory of rescuing the Prime Minister to others.

As we drew up, Major Norman jumped out, and a plain-clothes man took his place. He conferred with Poirot for a few minutes, and then went off briskly.

I, too, jumped out, and caught Poirot by the arm.
"I congratulate you, old fellow! They have told you the hiding-place? But, look here, you must wire to France at once. You'll be too late if you go yourself."

Poirot looked at me curiously for a minute or two.
"Unfortunately, my friend, there are some things that cannot be sent by telegram."

• □ • □ • □ •

At that moment Major Norman returned, accompanied by a young officer in the uniform of the Flying Corps.
"This is Captain Lyall, who will fly you over to France. He can start at once."
"Wrap up warmly, Sir," said the young pilot. "I can lend you a coat, if you like."

Poirot was consulting his enormous watch. He murmured to himself: "Yes, there is time—just time." Then he looked up, and bowed politely to the young officer.

"I thank you, Monsieur. But it is not I who am your passenger. It is this gentleman here."

He moved a little aside as he spoke, and a figure came forward out of the darkness. It was the second male prisoner who had gone in the other car, and as the light fell on his face, I gave a gasp of surprise.

It was the Prime Minister!

IV.

"For heaven's sake, tell me all about it," I cried impatiently, as Poirot, Norman, and I motored back to London. "How in the world did they manage to smuggle him back to England?"

"There was no need to smuggle him back," replied Poirot drily. "The Prime Minister has never left England. He was kidnapped on his way from Windsor to London."
"What?"

"I will make all clear. The Prime Minister was in his car, his secretary beside him. Suddenly a pad of chloroform is clapped on his face——"

"But by whom?"

"By the clever linguistic Captain Daniels. As soon as the Prime Minister is unconscious, Daniels picks up the speaking-tube, and directs O'Murphy to turn to the right, which the chauffeur, quite unsuspicious, does. A few yards down that unfrequented road, a large car is standing, apparently broken down. Its driver signals to O'Murphy to stop. O'Murphy slows up. The stranger approaches. Daniels leans out of the window, and, probably with the aid of an instantaneous anæsthetic, such as ethyl-chloride, the chloroform trick is repeated. In a few seconds, the two helpless men are dragged out and transferred to the other car, and a pair of substitutes take their places."

"Impossible!"

"Pas du tout! Have you not seen music-hall turns imitating celebrities with marvellous accuracy? Nothing is easier than to personate a public character. The Prime Minister of England is far easier to understudy than Mr. John Smith of Clapham, say. As for O'Murphy's 'double,' no one was going to take much notice of him until after the departure of the Prime Minister, and by then he would have made himself scarce. He drives straight from Charing Cross to the meeting-place of his friends. He goes in as O'Murphy, he emerges as someone quite different. O'Murphy has disappeared, leaving a conveniently suspicious trail behind him."

"But the man who personated the Prime Minister was seen by everyone!"

"He was not seen by anyone who knew him privately or intimately. And Daniels shielded him from contact with anyone as much as possible. Moreover, his face was bandaged up, and anything unusual in his manner would be put down to the fact that he was suffering from shock as a result of the attempt upon his life. Mr. MacAdam has a weak throat, and always spares his voice as much as possible before any great speech. The deception was perfectly easy to keep up as far as France. There it would be impracticable and impossible — so the Prime Minister disappears. The police of this country hurry across the Channel, and no one bothers to go into the details of the first attack. To sustain the illusion that the abduction has taken place in France, Daniels is gagged and chloroformed in a convincing manner."

"And the man who has enacted the part of the Prime Minister?"

"Rids himself of his disguise. He and the bogus chauffeur may be arrested as suspicious characters, but no one will dream of suspecting their real part in the drama, and they will eventually be released for lack of evidence."

"And the real Prime Minister?"

He and O'Murphy were driven straight to the house of 'Mrs. Everard,' at Hampstead, Daniels' so-called 'aunt.' In reality, she is Frau Bertha Ebenthal, and the police have been looking for her for some time. It is a valuable little present that I have made to them—to say nothing of Daniels! Ah, it was a clever plan, but he did not reckon on the cleverness of Hercule Poirot!"

I think my friend might well be excused his moment of vanity. "When did you first begin to suspect the truth of the matter?" "When I began to work the right way—from within! I could not make that shooting affair fit in—but when I saw that the net result of it was that the Prime Minister went to France with his face bound up, I began to comprehend! And when I visited all the cottage hospitals between Windsor and London, and found that no one answering to my description had had his face bound up and dressed that morning, I was sure! After that, it was child's-play for a mind like mine!"

V.

The following morning, Poirot showed me a telegram he had just received. It had no place of origin, and was unsigned.

It ran: "In time."

Later in the day the evening papers published an account of the Allied Conference. They laid particular stress on the magnificent ovation accorded to Mr. David MacAdam, whose inspiring speech had produced a deep and lasting impression.

THE END.

Made in United States
North Haven, CT
03 March 2022

16705525R00050